MOUSEKIN'S ABC

VERSE AND PICTURES BY EDNA MILLER

*Book Nook
Pattison School*

Simon and Schuster Books for Young Readers
Published by Simon & Schuster Inc., New York

To Mark Joseph

Copyright © 1972 by Edna Miller
All rights reserved including the right
of reproduction in whole or in part in any form.
Published by Simon and Schuster Books for Young Readers
A Division of Simon & Schuster, Inc.
Simon & Schuster Building
Rockefeller Center
1230 Avenue of the Americas
New York, NY 10020

10 9 8 7 6 5 4 3 2

(pbk) 20 19 18 17 16 15 14 13 12 11

Simon and Schuster Books for Young Readers
is a trademark of Simon & Schuster, Inc.
Manufactured in the United States of America

Library of Congress Cataloging-in-Publication Data
Miller, Edna, 1920–
Mousekin's ABC.
Summary: As a mouse journeys through the forest,
he investigates something for each letter of the
alphabet—acorns, bats, cottontails, etc.
[1. Nature—Fiction. 2. Alphabet. 3. Stories in rhyme
I. Title. PZ8.3.M6133Mo 1988 [E] 88-6556
ISBN 0-671-66472-7   ISBN 0-671-66473-5 PBK

A is for acorns Mousekin has found
under the oak tree, ripe on the ground.
Some he will eat and some he will store.
When the snow falls, he'll find no more.

B is for bat.
He's little and brown
and when he's asleep
he hangs upside down.
He has 38 teeth
and a small pug nose.
He's hunting for insects
wherever he goes.

C is for cottontail
born in a nest
that his mother had lined
with the fur from her breast.
Now he is grown
and deep in the clover.
Mousekin has seen him
when night is over.

D is for daisies,
dandelions too.
Mousekin discovered
a place where they grew.
There he saw a duck and a drake
swimming along on a bright summer lake.

E is for ermine,
white in the snow,
but the tip of his tail
is black as a crow.
Mousekin has spied him
and hides way up high
so the hungry young ermine
passes him by.

F is for fawn in the firefly light
asleep in forest, hidden from sight.
He'll stay with his mother for nearly a year
then go off on his own as a fully-grown deer.

G is for goose,
who nests on the ground
and flies through the air
with a loud honking sound.
When goldenrod blooms
and bright summer ends
the goose will fly south
in a gaggle of friends.

H is for hawk
swooping down from the hill —
a streak in the sky
going straight for his kill.
Mousekin dives into
the hawthorn tree hollow
and the long-legged hare
will be quick to follow.

I is for insects that whistle and sing.
Creepy ones, crawly ones,
insects that sting.
With transparent wings
they fly through the air.
Although they are tiny
you know they are there.

J is for jay
in the jewelweed,
scolding small birds
who are looking for feed.

Mousekin peeks out of
a jack-in-the-pulpit
and frightens away
the feathery culprit.

K is for katydids singing their song.
They sing about Katy all night long.
"Katy did! Katy didn't!"
they call to and fro.
(Who is this Katy and what do they know?)

L is for lilies
that grow near a brook,
and brighten the corner
of some shady nook.

M is for Mousekin,
  eyes shining bright,
  searching for food
  in the forest at night.
  With the first light of dawn
  and the first robin's call,
  he curls up to sleep
  in a soft furry ball.

N is for nest Mousekin has found
snug in a tree, away from the ground.
When four robins hatch
and four robins fly,
Mousekin can nest in this home in the sky.

O is for owl
in the moon's shining light
hunting his food
in swift, soundless flight.
Mousekin will watch
and Mousekin will hear —
a mouse darts for cover
should screech owl appear.

P is for polliwog
in the pond weed
swimming about
through willow and reed.
Soon he'll be growing
front feet and hind
and losing his tail:
A frog you will find.

Q is for quail huddled together—
tight in a ring, no matter the weather.
Should hunters or dogs or red fox come near,
in a loud whirrrrr of wings they'll all disappear.

R for raccoons in moonlit places
who steal through the night
with masks on their faces.
Four furry rascals,
eyes all agleam,
washing their food in a cool running stream.

S is for scarecrow
stuffed full of straw,
shooing the blackbirds.
Hear how they caw!
He's dressed like a man.
His coat is bright red.
Mousekin thinks scarecrow
would make a nice bed.

T is for turtle with no need to hide.
When dark clouds appear, he's safely inside.
He pulls in his head, tucks in his feet—
snug in his shell, his house is complete.

U is for umbrellas
found in the woods—
bright little toadstools
with waterproof hoods.

V is for violets,
a beautiful sight,
deep vivid purples
and velvety whites.
Down in the valley
they're dotted with dew.
Mousekin has stopped to nibble a few.

W is for woodchuck
in the wild grasses
eating his fill
before summer passes.
He goes underground
in the month of October
and sleeps safely there
until winter is over.

X can be seen
in paths that cross
deep in the forest
where tall trees toss.

Y is for yellow jackets
near bright yellow petals.
Mousekin will move
if the stinging wasps settle.

Z is for zephyr
a soft gentle breeze,
that blows through the forest
and rustles the leaves.
The sounds awake Mousekin
asleep in a tree,
for some new adventure
from A to Z.